The Pet Potato

Josh Lacey   Momoko Abe

Andersen Press

All Albert wanted was a pet.
But his mum and dad always said no.

They said, "We're too busy for a dog."

For Esther.
I promised you a puppy, and you're still waiting. I'm sorry!
Will you accept this book instead? – J.L.

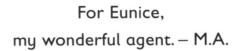

For Eunice,
my wonderful agent. – M.A.

First published in Great Britain in 2022 by Andersen Press Ltd.,

20 Vauxhall Bridge Road, London SW1V 2SA, UK

Vijverlaan 48, 3062 HL Rotterdam, Nederland

Text copyright © Josh Lacey 2022.

Illustration copyright © Momoko Abe 2022.

The rights of Josh Lacey and Momoko Abe to be identified as the

author and illustrator of this work have been asserted

by them in accordance with the Copyright, Designs and Patents Act, 1988.

All rights reserved.

Printed and bound in China.

1   3   5   7   9   10   8   6   4   2

British Library Cataloguing in Publication Data available.

ISBN 978 1 83913 080 9

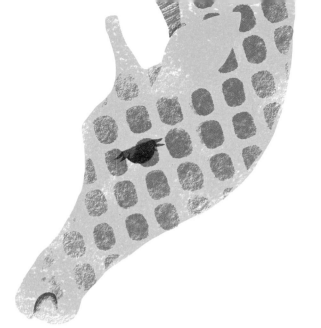

They said, "Cats make Mum sneeze."

They said, "Rabbits need a big garden."

They said, "Of course we can't have a giraffe! Don't be silly."

Albert never gave up. There was nothing else he wanted for Christmas or his birthday.

Morning and evening,

he begged his parents for a pet.

Until one day Dad called him over and said, "I have a present for you."

It was a small parcel wrapped up in blue paper and tied with a piece of ribbon.

"What's this?" Albert said. "There's only one way to find out," Dad said.

Albert opened the parcel and inside he found

a potato.

"You wanted a pet," Dad said. "There you go."
"That is not a pet," Albert said. "That is a potato."
"It's a pet potato," Dad said.

Dad made jokes like that all the time. Albert had learnt to
ignore them. He put the potato away and forgot about it.

Potatoes can't look sad.

Or lonely.

But somehow this one did.

Albert laid out his train tracks.

When he had finished, the potato went for
a ride in one of the carriages.

Albert built a tower with a room at the top.
From there the potato could see for miles around.

Albert took the potato to the playground.

It swung on the swings,

and rolled down the slide,

and went

round and

round and

round the roundabout.

Mickey wanted to use
the potato as a football,
but Albert said no. That
wouldn't be nice.

Potatoes aren't allowed in swimming pools, so it had to stay with Mum while Albert had his lesson.

When they went to the library, Albert and the potato took turns to choose.

For some reason, the potato particularly liked books about pirates.

When Albert had his bath, the potato sat on the edge of the tub.

After bath time it listened to his stories.

That night, the potato slept on his pillow.

On Sunday morning, the potato disappeared.

Albert searched his room, but it
was nowhere to be seen.

It wasn't playing with the trains.

Or up in the tower.
It might have gone for a walk.
Or down to the shop to buy some milk.

But potatoes can't really do that.
Can they?

He found his potato in the rubbish.
"Put it back, please," Mum said.
Albert refused. "You can't throw
him away!"
"It's smelly and mouldy," Mum said.
"It's going green. I don't
want that thing in
my house."

Dad dug a hole.
Albert put his potato
in the ground.

They covered him up.

They said goodbye.

Mum and Dad sat down with Albert for a serious talk.
"You were so good at looking after the potato," Mum
said. "We think you're ready for a real pet." Dad said,
"We're going to get you a hamster."

But Albert didn't want a hamster.
Nor did he want a dog, a cat, a rabbit, or even a giraffe.
He wanted his own pet back.
His beautiful, perfect pet.

POTATO

After a couple of weeks
a little shoot appeared.

The shoot grew leaves.

Dad gave the fork to Albert.

Albert dug.

Every day, the leaves were bigger.

And dug.

Until he found all the potatoes.

There were enough for everyone.